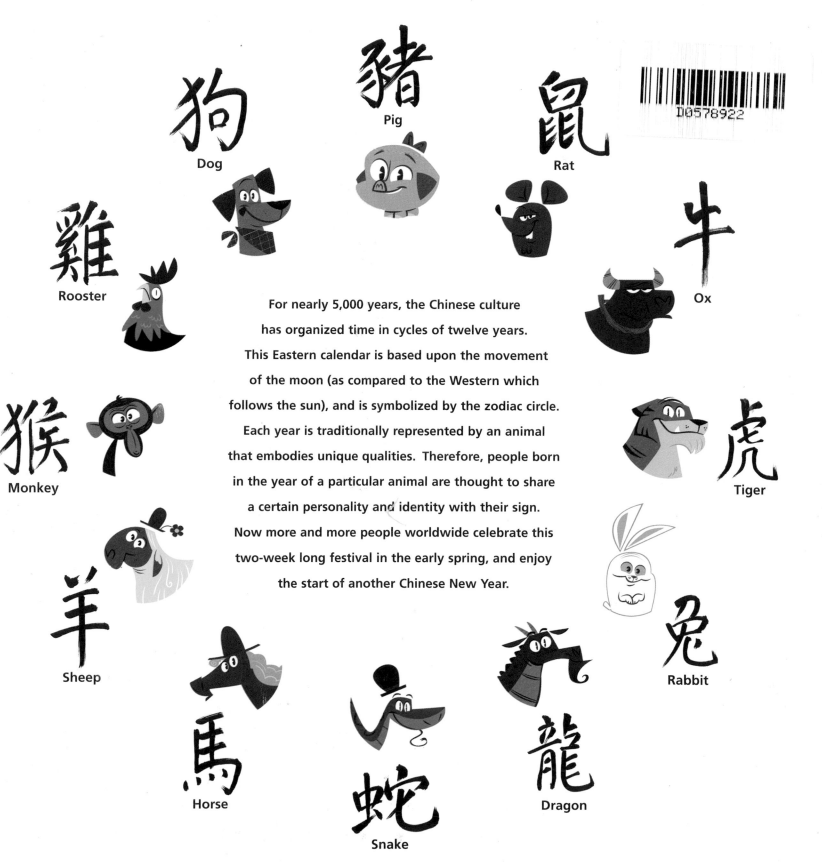

豬
Pig

狗
Dog

鼠
Rat

牛
Ox

雞
Rooster

虎
Tiger

猴
Monkey

羊
Sheep

兔
Rabbit

馬
Horse

蛇
Snake

龍
Dragon

For nearly 5,000 years, the Chinese culture has organized time in cycles of twelve years. This Eastern calendar is based upon the movement of the moon (as compared to the Western which follows the sun), and is symbolized by the zodiac circle. Each year is traditionally represented by an animal that embodies unique qualities. Therefore, people born in the year of a particular animal are thought to share a certain personality and identity with their sign. Now more and more people worldwide celebrate this two-week long festival in the early spring, and enjoy the start of another Chinese New Year.

D0578922

To my sister, Pamela, who has always shown the way.
—O.C.

To Alli, Jacob, Owen, and baby Emma. Without your love, encouragement, sacrifice, and inspiration, these illustrations wouldn't have been possible. I'm truly blessed to have you as my family and love you all very much.
—J.A.

immedium
Immedium, Inc.   P.O. Box 31846   San Francisco, CA 94131
www.immedium.com

First hardcover edition published 2006.

Edited by Don Menn
Book design by Elaine Chu
Calligraphy by Lucy Chu

Printed in Singapore
10 9 8 7 6 5 4 3 2 1

Chin, Oliver Clyde, 1969-
   The year of the pig : tales from the Chinese zodiac / written by
Oliver Chin ; illustrated by Miah Alcorn. -- 1st hardcover ed.
      p. cm.
   Summary: Patty the piglet learns what her best qualities really are
when Farmer Wu needs everyone's help to find a lost ring. Lists
the birth years and characteristics of individuals born in the Chinese
Year of the Pig.
   ISBN-13: 978-1-59702-007-7 (hardcover)
   [1. Pigs--Fiction. 2. Animals--Infancy--Fiction. 3. Domestic
animals--Fiction. 4. Astrology, Chinese--Fiction.]   I. Alcorn, Miah,
ill. II. Title.
PZ7.C44235Ye 2006
[E]--dc22

2006017864
ISBN: 1-59702-007-9

The Year of the Pig

Tales from the Chinese Zodiac

Written by Oliver Chin

Illustrated by Miah Alcorn

immedium
Immedium, Inc.
San Francisco

SQUEAL!

At dawn, a joyful squeal rang
through the farmyard. A new day
had just begun, so Farmer Wu woke up
and walked out to his barn. Inside Mama
and Papa Pig just had a baby!

The piglet was small and soft,
but had a well-bred look about her.
Farmer Wu smiled as he cradled
the newest member of his farm.
Mama and Papa named her "Patricia"
or "Patty" for short.

All the neighbors wanted to see the baby. Big and small, they crowded around the pigpen.

They congratulated Mama and Papa and cooed at little Patty.

Mama whispered in Patty's ear,
"These are your uncles,
aunts, and cousins."

Papa added, "Listen to your
elders, because they know
what is best for you."

Delighted, Patty clapped her
hooves, "Yay!"

Quickly Patty learned the lay of the land. Mama showed her where the farmer's family and the other animals lived.

Then Papa taught her all their names and duties.

Everyone admired how Patty was such a fast learner.
"What's next for me to study?" Patty asked eagerly.

So a few of them agreed that it was time to teach her
some manners.

Patty's parents liked to roll in the mud, especially to cool off on hot days.

Next door, Auntie Sheep shook her head and advised Patty, "You should keep your skin clean, just like my wool."

"But getting dirty is really fun," replied Patty.

She enjoyed **SLIDING!**

SLIPPING!

and sitting on the soft wet earth. Nothing felt better than a good mud bath!

Mama and Papa loved mealtime when Farmer Wu would fill their trough. Nearby, Uncle Ox flicked his tail and instructed Patty,

"You should chew slowly and not make a mess."

"But food smells too tasty," explained Patty.

When she got hungry, Patty hurried to join her parents and dived face first into her chow.

After every meal, Patty looked very sloppy indeed.

At night, Patty's parents nestled beside each other and snored loudly. Auntie Horse pawed at the ground and told Patty,

"You should sleep standing up and not be so noisy."

"But lying down feels so good," sighed Patty.

At bedtime, Patty would always squeeze in between her parents. Warm and snug, Patty would slumber up a storm.

Patty liked her pigpen. But other animals got to wander about the farm, and Patty wanted to explore as well.

She nudged the gate with her snout, but it wouldn't budge.

Strolling by, Cousin Dog
grinned and shook
his head.

He warned her, "Be content to stay where you are
and leave the roaming to others."

Patty snorted in disagreement
and curled her tail.

Then one morning, Farmer Wu shouted, "Ai Ya! Where did it go?"

He had lost his valuable jade ring!

Soon the whole farm buzzed with excitement.

Patty rooted around the pen, but didn't find anything.

Cousin Dog laughed, "Don't worry. This is my job, so just sit back and watch."

Off Cousin Dog went. He sniffed Farmer Wu's hand and began hunting for the missing jade ring.

Patty shouted, "I want to help too!" But she could only watch anxiously from her pigpen.

All day long, Farmer Wu and Cousin Dog ran around the farm. Patty thought, "I bet they will find his ring soon."

But alas, after a long day of looking, they had no luck!

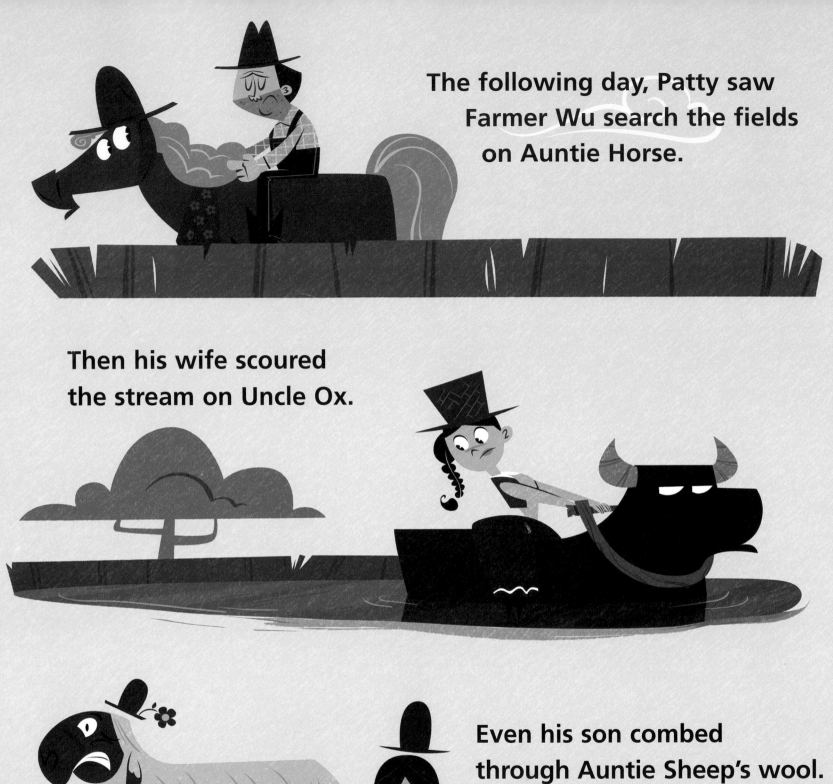

The following day, Patty saw Farmer Wu search the fields on Auntie Horse.

Then his wife scoured the stream on Uncle Ox.

Even his son combed through Auntie Sheep's wool.

But the ring was nowhere to be found. Finally Mama suggested, "Patty, you should help them."

Papa encouraged her, "Yes, we know that you can do it."

So Patty thought of a plan!

That night, as Cousin Dog stood watch,
Patty dozed off and started to snore loudly.

"Why can't you sleep right?" whined
Auntie Horse.

But Patty kept on snoring.

Watching Patty enjoy her sleep, a tired Cousin Dog decided to get some rest too.

But when he left, Patty opened her eyes and tiptoed closer to the pigpen's gate.

Then Patty rolled on the ground and coated herself with mud. "Why are you getting so dirty?" bleated Auntie Sheep.

Next Patty crouched as low as she could under the gate's bottom rail.

She squeezed, squeaked, and slithered. Finally she slipped out!

POP!

Auntie Horse and Sheep gasped with surprise.

Curious to learn what Patty was up to, Uncle Ox tagged along.

In his haste, Farmer Wu had dropped one of his gloves outside her pen. After sniffing it, Patty noticed something else in the air,

"That is a strange smell."

So Patty followed the scent.

Around the corner of the barn, she found the farm's compost heap. It was piled high with leftover plants and vegetables of all sorts. "Why are you still so hungry?" grunted Uncle Ox.

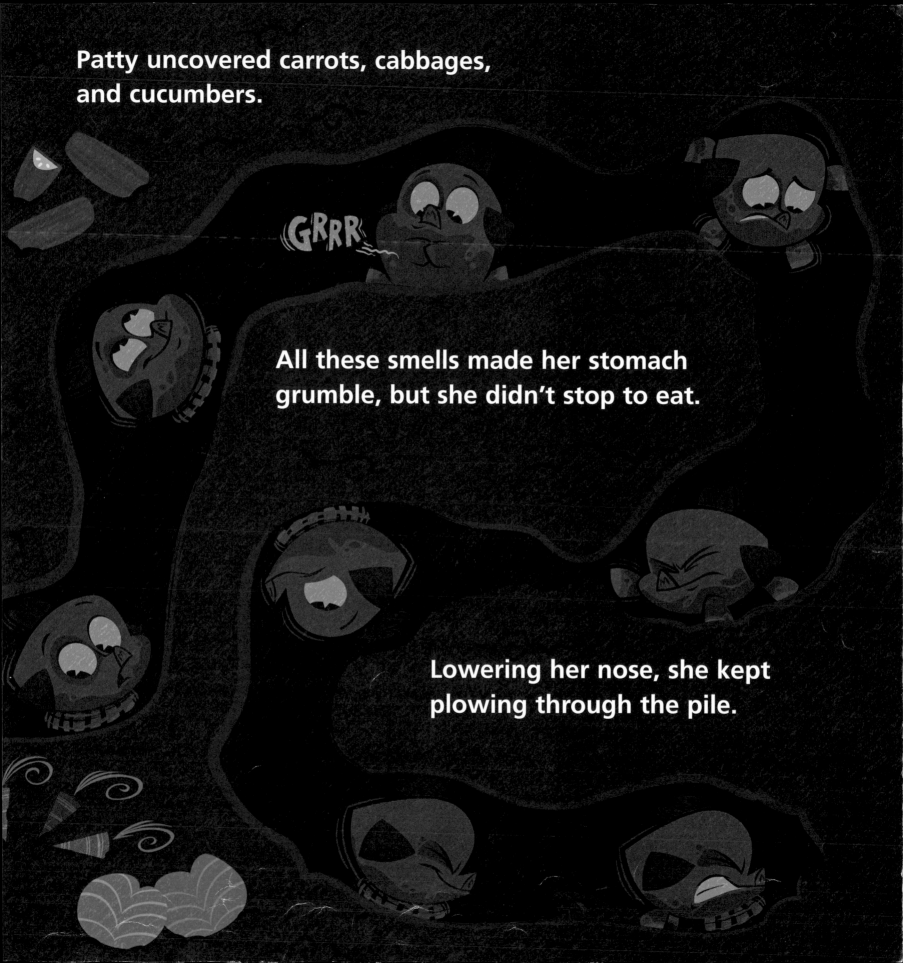

Patty uncovered carrots, cabbages, and cucumbers.

All these smells made her stomach grumble, but she didn't stop to eat.

Lowering her nose, she kept plowing through the pile.

Finally Patty discovered something that wasn't food at all.

She squealed, "I've found it!"

Hearing her cry, everybody rushed out to the barn.

Afterwards, Farmer Wu would let Patty
out of the pen wherever she pleased.
Patty even got to go into the house as
long as she took a bath beforehand.

Mama and Papa Pig were proud of their little piglet. No one complained anymore about Patty's manners, and everyone agreed it was a remarkable Year of the Pig.

Pig

1911, 1923, 1935, 1947, 1959, 1971, 1983, 1995, 2007, 2019

People born in the Year of the Pig are warm, sociable, and sincere.
They are resilient, inquisitive, and intelligent. But they can be impulsive, sensitive,
and stubborn. Though they may seem to take their time and enjoy themselves,
the generosity and courage of pigs are qualities to treasure!